COUNTING DINOS

Eric Pinder   pictures by **Junissa Bianda**

Albert Whitman & Company
Chicago, Illinois

D0001482

Rodrigo was a dinosaur
who tried to count from one to four.
He started off with number one.
One tree, one pond, one cloud, one sun—

one tail he liked to swing for fun!

Another dinosaur named Sue
said, "I can help you count to two!
I have two arms, two pairs of claws,
but more than two teeth in my jaws!"

She saw two clouds up in the sky,
two *pterodactyls* flying by.
"How many wings? They each have two.
Now what comes next? I know. Do you?"

Another dinosaur named Stan
said, "I can count to three. I can!
Just look at me. I have three horns!"

3

He snacked on branches full of thorns.
And on one branch, a nice surprise,
he counted three big dragonflies!

A funny dinosaur named Gus
said, "I can count the four of us—
Rodrigo, Stan, and Gus and Sue.
I know what all of us can do...
Let's count the spikes upon my tail!"

He had four spikes and four big feet.
He found four stones—a yummy treat!
"We know the numbers up to four.
But what comes next? Let's count some more!"

The smartest dinosaurs alive
came running in a pack of five.

"We love to count," they said. "It's true.
If we can count, then so can you!"

They found five pine cones on the ground,
five mossy boulders in a mound.

Another smart one joined the mix.
She laughed and said, "Let's count to six!"
Six dragonflies with blurry wings.
Six itty-bitty furry things.

But when the dinos tried to play,
the little creatures ran away!

A hungry dinosaur named Kevin
taught the rest to count to seven.

He munched on seven leaves for lunch.
His great big jaws went crunch, crunch, crunch.

A clever dinosaur named Kate
said, "Guess what's next? The number eight!"
She left eight footprints on the beach.

She saw eight fish just out of reach.
"The number eight," said Kate, "is fine...

8

but even better's number nine!"
She found nine shells with loops and swirls.
Inside nine clamshells—lots of pearls!

9

Rodrigo cheered. He said, "It's fun to count to nine. But are we done?"

The smartest dinos, once again,
came running in a pack of ten.
"Don't stop yet. We'll show you how
to count to ten. Let's start right now!"

The fastest one said, "Follow me!"

What did they count? What did they see?

One river flowing to the shore.
Two big volcanoes. Hear them roar!

Three comets shining in the sky.
Four *pterodactyls* flying high.

Five happy, buzzing, busy bees.
Six enormous redwood trees.

5

6

7

Seven seed cones on the ground.
"And guess what else we all have found?"

Eight furry mammals, way down low.
Nine leafy ferns, all in a row.

And standing up on tiny legs,
ten babies hatching from their eggs!
And as those hatchlings grew and grew...

Rodrigo taught them numbers too!

Life in Dinosaur Times

Rodrigo, his friends, and the other living things in this book are based on real plants and animals that have lived on Earth. Can you spot the one below that is still around today?

Ankylosaurus

Ankylosaurus had a bony body with knobs and plates. The large club at the end of its tail helped protect *Ankylosaurus* from bigger dinosaurs.

Tyrannosaurus rex

Tyrannosaurus rex was a dinosaur with terrible teeth and teeny-tiny arms. T. rex used its strong jaws and sharp teeth to catch its food.

Triceratops

Triceratops is named for the three big horns it had on its head. *Triceratops* munched on ancient trees called cycads, which had long, thorny leaves.

Dragonfly

Dragonflies have been around for a long time—even before there were dinosaurs! The first dragonflies were much larger than they are today. Extra oxygen in the air helped these insects grow to the size of seagulls! Over the ages, dragonflies have gotten smaller.

Stegosaurus

Stegosaurus had tiny teeth. Like other plant eaters, *Stegosaurus* sometimes swallowed stones and pebbles to help grind up its food. This dinosaur had big, thin plates on its back and a tail with spikes.

Pterodactyl

Pterodactyl had a long beak and wide wings. It looked like a mix between a dinosaur and a bird, but it was neither. It was actually a flying reptile!

Troodon

Troodon was a small dinosaur with big eyes and a big brain. It may have been the smartest dinosaur of all! Fossils show us that *Troodon* laid large numbers of eggs in nests, and that other smart, quick dinosaurs, like *Deinonychus* and *Velociraptor*, roamed in packs.

Apatosaurus

Apatosaurus was one of the biggest dinosaurs—bigger than a bus! It used its long neck to snack on high-up leaves that other plant eaters couldn't reach.

Spinosaurus

Spinosaurus was probably the only dinosaur that liked to swim. It had a long snout like a crocodile's, and it liked to eat fish.

Ammonite

Ammonites were squid-like creatures. As they grew, the shells they lived in got bigger too. Ammonites moved through the water by sucking in water and squirting it back out.

Deltatheridium

Deltatheridium was a small mammal that lived during dinosaur times. It may be related to today's opossums and kangaroos.

For Erynn, who knows that every word counts—EP

For Krisna—JB

Library of Congress Cataloging-in-Publication data is on file with the publisher.

Text copyright © 2018 by Eric Pinder
Pictures copyright © 2018 by Albert Whitman & Company
Pictures by Junissa Bianda
First published in the United States of America in 2018 by Albert Whitman & Company
ISBN 978-0-8075-1281-4

Printed in China
10 9 8 7 6 5 4 3 2 1 WKT 22 21 20 19 18

For more information about Albert Whitman & Company,
visit our website at www.albertwhitman.com.